Do You Love Someone?

JOAN WALSH ANGLUND

Do

You

Love

Someone?

HARCOURT BRACE JOVANOVICH, INC., NEW YORK

BY JOAN WALSH ANGLUND

A Friend Is Someone Who Likes You
The Brave Cowboy
Look Out the Window
Love Is a Special Way of Feeling
In a Pumpkin Shell
Cowboy and His Friend
Christmas Is a Time of Giving
Nibble Nibble Mousekin
Spring Is a New Beginning
Cowboy's Secret Life
The Joan Walsh Anglund Sampler
A Pocketful of Proverbs
Childhood Is a Time of Innocence
Un Ami, C'est Quelqu'un Qui T'aime
A Book of Good Tidings
What Color Is Love?
A Year Is Round
A Is for Always
Amor Est Sensus Quidam Peculiaris
Morning Is a Little Child
A Packet of Pictures
The Little Bookshelf
Do You Love Someone?

FOR ADULTS

A Cup of Sun
A Slice of Snow

B C D E F G H I J
ISBN 0-15-224190-6
Library of Congress Catalog Card Number: 76-152692
Printed in the United States of America

for bob

with my love

The universe is wide and wonderful
and filled with many stars.

The world is rich and varied
and filled with many people.

And among its
  hundreds of towns,
    and thousands of homes,
      and millions of people,
each of us
  is only ''one'' . . .

one small person
  in a world
    of millions of other people,
  in a universe
    of billions of other worlds.

Knowing this,
    sometimes we each feel very small.
Sometimes we feel lonely and lost,
    as though nothing we do
        can ever truly matter.

Each of us

wants to be needed.

Each of us
wants to be remembered.

Each of us
  wants to be important
    in his own special way.

There are many different ways
to be important in this world.

Some people become doctors
and heal the sick.

Some become farmers
and feed the hungry.

And some become teachers
and share wisdom and knowledge.

But you can be a shepherd,
or a shoemaker,
or a baker,
or a barber,
or a captain,
or a carpenter,
or a king!
And whatever you are,
there is still one thing
that matters most.

Do you love someone . . .
  and does someone love you?

For the heart
  is its own world,
and in that world
  you are important!

And that's what really matters,
isn't it?